llama llama
time to share

Anna Dewdney

SCHOLASTIC INC.

Llama Llama playing trains,
driving trucks, and flying planes.

Someone's at the door . . . who is it?
Brand new neighbors come to visit.

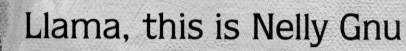

Llama, this is Nelly Gnu

Look!

She has a dolly, too.

Mrs. Gnu, would you like tea?

Come and have a cup with me.

You two kids can play in there. . . .

And Llama,
  don't forget to **share.**

Trains and trucks and puzzles, too.
What's the Gnu girl want to do?
Play with kitchen? Build with blocks?
Llama opens up his box.

Nelly starts to build a town.
Llama Llama starts to frown. . . .

Nelly Gnu makes walls and stairs.
Llama watches from a chair.

Nelly stacks the blocks up high.
Fuzzy Llama wants to try.

It's a castle! Make it tall.
Fuzzy Llama jumps the wall!

Build a tower. Make a moat.
Nelly's dolly rows a boat.

What can Llama Llama add?
Maybe sharing's **not** so bad.

Little baby Gnu makes noise.
Mrs. Gnu gets jingly toys.
Baby screams and kicks his feet.
Mama thinks it's time to eat.

Moms are talking,
baby's chewing. . . .

Where's that Gnu girl?
What's **she** doing?

Oh, **disaster!** Dolly drama!

Nelly Gnu has
Fuzzy Llama!

He's not hers! This isn't fair!

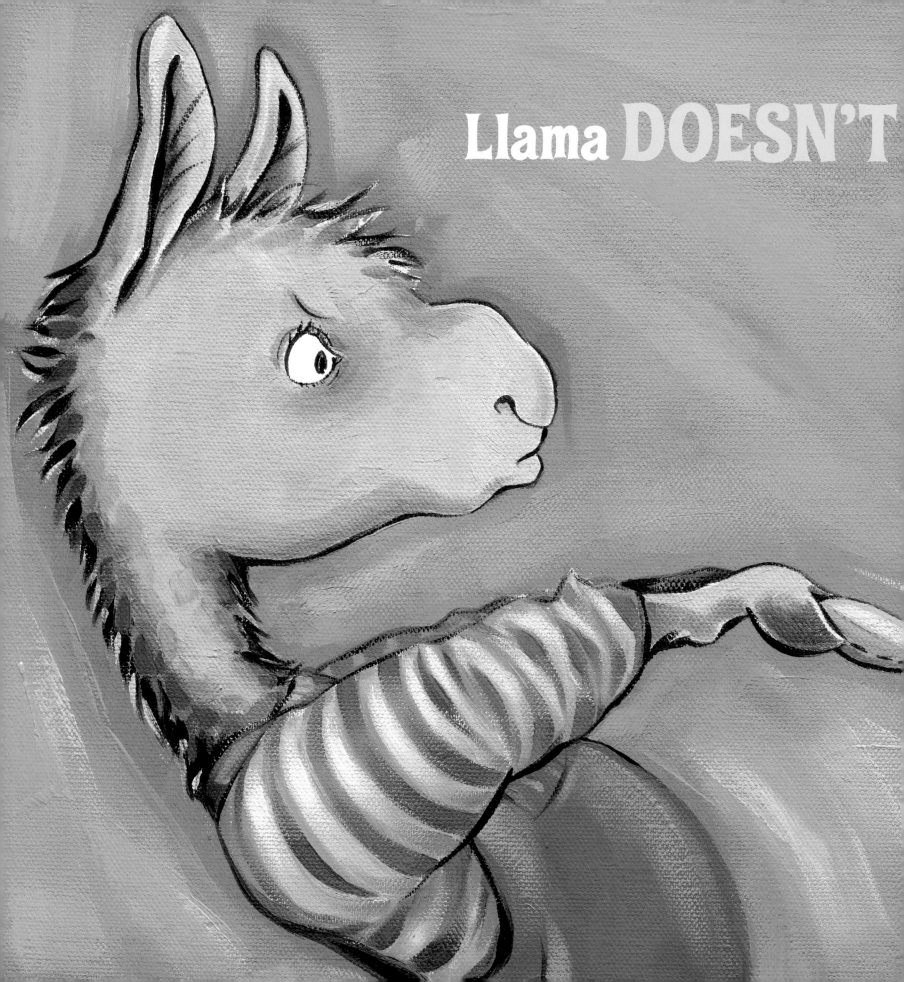

Llama DOESN'T

Fuzzy Llama ripped in two . . .
all because of Nelly Gnu!

It's a **llama-mergency!**

Mama! Fix his arm
for me!

A bit of thread and good as new . . .
but this is what we're going to do:

I'll put Fuzzy on the stairs
until you're **sure** that you can share.

Nelly's sorry.
Llama, too.

It's time for
something
else to do.

Maybe tractors?

Maybe not.

Like to dress up?

Not a lot.

Let's play kitchen!
Make a cake!

Nelly mixes. Llama bakes.

Look—our fancy cake is done!

Hmmm . . .
what would make this game **more** fun?

Fuzzy Llama, on the stairs!

Llama thinks it's **time to share.**

Playtime's over. It's the end . . .

but Llama has a brand new friend.

Nelly will be back,
and then . . .

Llama wants to
share again!

To my sister Alice, with love

ISBN 978-0-545-78928-8

12 11 10 9 8 7 6 5 4 3 2   14 15 16 17 18 19/0

Printed in the U.S.A.   08

This edition first printing, September 2014

Set in ITC Quorum
The art for this book was created with oil paint, colored pencil, and oil pastel on primed canvas.